DENNIS the MENACE

THE ULTIMATE MENACE!

BEANObooks

published under licence by

meadowside
CHILDREN'S BOOKS

DENNIS THE VENTRILOQUIST

"You can't be serious?" Dennis gasped.

He staggered backwards in shock and bumped into Dad, who was blocking the exit. Mum glared at Dennis with her hands on her hips.

"I'm as serious as a stink bomb in a broken lift," she said.

Dennis couldn't help but grin. That was one of his all-time favourite menaces.

Even Dad started to look nervous.

"Do you think this is really such a good idea?" he asked, chewing on his nails.

"I won't have any more running

2

around, menacing everyone in Beanotown!" Mum insisted. "This summer, Dennis is going to get a job!"

"NO WAY!" came a shout from the window.

Curly and Pie Face had been waiting for Dennis and they had heard everything. Mum and Dad turned to look at them, and Dennis slipped past Dad and zoomed out of the house on his skateboard.

"Good timing, lads!" he yelled as he shot past them. "Come on, we've got some menacing to do!"

Before Mum could reach the door, Dennis, Curly and Pie Face had disappeared around the corner at the end of the street.

"Do you reckon your mum's serious about you getting a job this summer?" asked Curly half an hour later.

The three of them were sitting on top of the bridge over the canal path with a large supply of menacing gear.

"Nah," said Dennis, grabbing a water balloon as he saw the Colonel striding down the path. "Well, yeah, but only in her dreams!"

He aimed the water balloon and fired.

"ARGGGHHH!" bellowed the Colonel as ice-cold water rained down on him.

"SHOT!" Dennis cheered, punching the air.

"You pack of menaces!" the Colonel roared, shaking his fist at them.

"We were just checking your hat for leaks, Colonel!" Dennis said with a wide grin.

"I'll check you for leaks when I catch up with you, you young scallywag!" the Colonel retorted.

"Scarper!" Dennis cried.

The three boys skateboarded away from the enraged Colonel and zoomed into town, where Dennis stopped in front of a large poster on the town hall notice board.

"Look at this!" he exclaimed.

The poster was bright red with white letters that read:

TALENT QUEST!
Your favourite talent show is coming to Beanotown! Perform a talent in front of the judges to win a place on the TV show!

"Brilliant!" said Pie Face. "I'll do my party trick."

"What, stuffing ten pies in your mouth at once?" said Curly. "Does that qualify as a talent?"

"Well, what are you gonna do?" huffed Pie Face.

7

"I'm gonna drink a gallon of pop and make it come down my nose," said Curly. "That's a talent – it made Walter faint when he saw me do it!"

"They're both good for menacing softies, but they're not gonna impress the judges," said Dennis. "When it comes to talent, it's just like menaces – the old ones are the best."

"What do you mean?" asked Curly.

"Water balloons, stink bombs and whoopee cushions are guaranteed menace material," said Dennis with a wide grin. "And I'm gonna do a guaranteed talent that'll get me a place on the show."

"What are you gonna do?" asked Pie Face, wide-eyed.

"Never you mind," said Dennis. "Come on Gnasher, we've got work to do!"

That afternoon, the librarian of Beanotown Library had a terrible shock. She was writing a threatening letter to Billy Whizz about an overdue library book, when she looked up and saw Dennis standing on the opposite side of the counter.

"EEEK!" she cried, her hand flying to her mouth.

"Shhh," said Dennis, putting his finger over his lips. "This is a library, you know."

"Wh-wh-what do you w-w-want?" said the trembling librarian.

Her eyes flickered from side to side, searching for incoming water bombs.

"Can I borrow this book, please?" Dennis asked.

"Is it booby trapped?" asked the librarian, breaking into a cold sweat. "Have you hidden insects inside it? Will it explode when I touch it?"

"Now that would be an awesome menace," said Dennis thoughtfully. "Some other time, though. Right now, it's just a book and I really want to borrow it."

The librarian gingerly took the book and stamped it. She watched Dennis stroll out of the library with the book under his arm. Then she ran her hand over her brow.

"I may have to go home early," she said to herself. "I must be coming down with something. What does Dennis want with a book about ventriloquism?"

A short while later, in the garden shed, Dennis opened the book and looked at Gnasher.

"As soon as I've learned ventriloquism, you're gonna be Gnasher the Amazing Talking Dog," said Dennis.

"Gnash?" said Gnasher, backing away nervously with his paw to his throat.

"Ventriloquism isn't an operation, you mutt!" Dennis told him. "It means that I'm gonna learn to throw my voice. Then you'll sit beside me and it'll sound like you're talking to the judges. They'll love it!"

There were some very strange noises coming from the shed that night. Dennis's neighbours shuddered as

they listened to the unearthly groans, coughs and wheezes. Dennis's parents just shut the windows and turned up the TV.

"What we don't know can't worry us," said Mum.

The next morning, Dennis emerged from the shed wearing a wide grin. Gnasher was beside him, wearing earmuffs and looking very hungry.

"Cracked it!" said Dennis. "Now for a little bit of practice!"

Sergeant Slipper was walking his beat down the main street in Beanotown, puffing his chest out and feeling very important.

"Good morning, Sergeant Slipper!" called the lady who ran the garden centre.

"Good morning, Mrs Potts," said Sergeant Slipper as he passed the shop.

"You mad old fruitloop," added Sergeant Slipper's voice.

"Well really!" said Mrs Potts. "I've never been so insulted!"

"You should get out more," said Sergeant Slipper's voice.

Mrs Potts picked up a small potted fern and hurled it at Sergeant Slipper, knocking his hat off. He turned around and glared at Mrs Potts in amazement.

"It'll be a prickly cactus if you're rude to me again!" hollered Mrs Potts. "You puffed up nuisance!"

She stormed into her shop and banged the door shut. Sergeant Slipper picked up his hat, scratching his head in confusion.

Neither of them spotted someone in a red and black jumper lurking behind the shrubbery section.

Sergeant Slipper walked on, feeling very puzzled.

"Good morning, Slipper!" boomed the Colonel as he marched out of the paper shop.

"Good morning, Colonel," said Sergeant Slipper.

"Hurry home and play with your toy soldiers," added Sergeant Slipper's voice.

"I beg your pardon?" exclaimed the Colonel.

"Quack!" said Sergeant Slipper's voice. "You're crackers!"

The Colonel went pink with fury and smacked Sergeant Slipper around the head with his rolled-up newspaper, knocking his hat off.

"I know your boss!" the Colonel bellowed. "Keep a civil tongue in your head!"

"I didn't say anything!" roared Sergeant Slipper as the Colonel strode off.

Neither of them noticed someone in a pair of dirty, black boots skulking behind the post box.

The Colonel marched homewards in a fury.

"Lovely morning, Colonel," called the baker from his shop window.

"Get back inside and start baking, you lazy fellow, or I'll set the soldiers on you!" called the Colonel's voice.

"I'll teach you to call me names, you crazy old coot!" cried the baker,

hurling a currant bun at the Colonel.

The currant bun hit the Colonel's nose and one of the currants pinged him in the eye.

"What's the matter with everyone this morning?" he roared.

Neither of them saw someone with very muddy knees creeping off down an alleyway.

By the time Dennis's mum went out to do her shopping, Beanotown was in uproar.

It seemed as if Sergeant Slipper had insulted everyone on his beat. The owner of the sweet shop had thrown a bullseye at Walter's mumsy for calling him 'goat face'. Minnie was having a wrestling match with Fatty Fudge because she heard him say that she wasn't half the minx she used to be. Half the shopkeepers in the street were refusing to speak to the others, and the mayor was threatening to close Beanotown unless whoever had called him 'Bumface' owned up.

The only person not in the middle of an argument was Dennis. He was strolling through town with his hands in his pockets, whistling.

"I smell a rat," said Mum to herself.

She hurried home and rummaged under the stairs until she found the outfit she wore when she entered Dennis's room. She didn't go in very often, but she hadn't forgotten the time when she had walked in without a hat on and ended up covered in three pints of jelly and a very surprised squid. She strapped on the body armour, plonked the army helmet on her head and pulled on the metal gauntlets. Then she grabbed a broom, went upstairs, took a deep breath and opened Dennis's door.

It took a few moments for her eyes to grow accustomed to the greenish haze. She used the broom handle to open the curtains and peered around. Strange smells and worrying noises filled the air. Spiders scurried across the floor and something green

was bubbling in the corner. Mum pretended that she hadn't seen it and looked around for anything unusual. Suddenly her eyes gleamed. On top of a bag of dog biscuits was one thing that she had never seen in Dennis's room before.

A book!

Dennis burst through the front door and kick-flicked his skateboard into the corner.

"Lunchtime, Gnasher!" he grinned.

Gnasher gave a low growl and the hairs on the back of Dennis's neck suddenly stood up.

"My menacing radar's telling me we need to get out of here!" Dennis yelled.

But before he could turn around, Dad had shot out of the hall cupboard and grabbed him. He dragged Dennis into the sitting room.

"Gerroff!" Dennis bellowed. "Lemme go!"

Mum was standing in the sitting room with a book in her hand. Next to her was a tall man in wellies and a waxed jacket.

"I know what you've been up to, you menace!" said Mum, waving the book at Dennis.

"I was just practising my talent for the show!" Dennis roared. "I've been practising all morning!"

"I know!" Mum snapped. "The whole town is arguing because of you!"

"Is this going to cost me money?" asked Dad in a faint voice.

"Farmer Burly has a job for you," said Mum. "Since you enjoy throwing your voice so much, you can practise

25

it for the rest of the summer
– as a living scarecrow in Farmer
Burly's fields!"

"I'm so bored!" Dennis roared.

He had been doing the job for a day and a half. Farmer Burly had put him next to a haystack in the middle of four large fields, and it was Dennis's job to throw his voice into each field in turn and scare away the birds.

"I've got to get outta here," Dennis grumbled, leaning back against the haystack.

The talent show was that afternoon, and Dennis planned to be there. But Farmer Burly would be down there like a shot if he saw the birds landing on the fields. He had to think of some way to get away without anyone realising.

27

Just then, he heard a horrible sound. Someone was skipping along the path beside the field and singing.

"Daisy, Daisy, give me your answer do! I'm half crazy all for the love of you!"

"Bleuurrgghh," said Dennis. "There's only one softy who'd skip around singing stuff like that. Someone ought to stop him before he damages people's eardrums."

Then a menacing gleam entered Dennis's eyes, and he rubbed his hands together.

Walter was skipping down the path with a handful of buttercups when he heard something that made him stop in his tracks.

"Walter!" called a voice. "It's me, your darling Matilda-wilda!"

"What are you doing in the field?" asked Walter.

"I've found some pretty flowers — come and have a look!" called the voice of his girlfriend.

"But there are insects and worms in the field," said Walter, biting his nails. "It's a bit scary!"

"Just get in here!" said Matilda's voice, suddenly sounding rather rough.

Walter jumped and scurried into the field.

"Where are you, smoochums?" he called.

"Right here, softy features!" growled Dennis loudly.

He grabbed Walter and hoisted him up on to the top of the haystack.

"Let me down!" Walter wailed, covering his eyes and lying spread-eagled on the haystack. "It's too high! I'm going to be sick! WAAAHHH! Mumsy!"

"That racket should keep the birds away," said Dennis with a grin. "Keep up the good work, Walter!"

Dennis raced back along the path to Beanotown. He found Gnasher lurking outside the butcher's and together they hurried to the town hall, where the talent show auditions were being held. Dennis skidded to a halt at the front of the queue, scattering people left, right and centre. Unicycles flew into the air, magicians lost the doves from their hats and the majorettes dropped their batons on their toes.

"Next!" bellowed the doorman.

Dennis and Gnasher stepped inside and onto the stage. The three famous TV judges were sitting in a row in front of him. The lady judge was checking her makeup in a hand mirror. The judge next to her was nervously drumming his fingers on the table, and the head judge had large chunks of cotton wool in his ears.

"I told you it was a mistake to come here," said the head judge. "That last girl – Minnie? – I've never heard singing like that in my life. I think she's made my eardrums bleed."

"Let's just get on with it," snapped the other man. "Next we have the Beanotown majorettes."

"What have I done to deserve this?" groaned the head judge, burying his face in his hands.

Dennis stood in the middle of the stage with Gnasher beside him.

He looked down at the tripe hound and grinned. This was their moment of triumph! He cleared his throat and said the first line of his act.

Or at least . . . he tried to. But no sound came out at all. Dennis grabbed his throat and massaged it, but it was no use. After all the practice he had done around Beanotown, and then a day and a half of yelling at Farmer Burly's birds, not to mention imitating Matilda, he had completely lost his voice!

"Thank you very much," said the head judge. "It's a no. Goodbye!"

Dennis stomped off the stage and burst out of the town hall door so fast that he sent the majorettes flying for a second time. He shoved his hands in his pockets and walked home, moodily scuffing his boots against the pavement.

When he got home, the sitting room windows were open. Floating out of them he heard angry voices and a squeaky, wailing sort of sound. Dennis crept up to the window and peered in. He could see Farmer Burly and Walter's mumsy. Dennis's dad had his chequebook out and was writing a cheque with steam coming out of his ears. Walter was sitting in the corner with straw in his hair and his glasses hanging off one ear. Dennis and Gnasher exchanged a quick glance. Then they sped back down the garden path, out of the gate and along the road towards their secret den.

That's the great thing about Gnasher, Dennis thought as they made their escape. I don't have to speak for him to know what I'm thinking. Scarper!

THE MENACE IDENTITY

It was summer in Beanotown. Usually that meant that everyone got very hot and sweaty worrying about what menaces Dennis was going to get up to over the school holidays. But this year, something was different. The streets were filled with people carrying tents and huge rucksacks. All the people were wearing flowers in their hair. A large stage was being built in one of Farmer Burly's fields. Beanotown was having its very first music festival.

Dennis rode out to the field with Curly and Pie Face to see what was going on.

They skidded the bikes to a halt outside the field gate, spraying a tidal wave of sloppy mud into the faces of three people who were standing there.

"Dennis, you menace!" snapped a weedy voice.

It was Walter the Softy, glaring at Dennis as he scraped mud out of his ears and cleaned his glasses.

"You rotten thing!" wailed Bertie

Blenkinsop, who was next to him. "You've ruined my favourite beige cardigan.

"Nah, that's not ruined," chortled Dennis. "Now it's a beige cardigan with brown spots."

Curly and Pie Face snorted with laughter as the third softy, Spotty Perkins, pulled out a comb and smoothed down his hair.

"What are you doing here?" said Walter.

"We've come to check out the music festival," said Dennis, hopping off his bike and peering into the field.

Camper vans and tents were dotted all around the big stage. Everyone was stomping around in wellies, getting muddy. It looked like there were no rules and no adults in charge. The whiff of hotdogs, hamburgers and fried onions reached Dennis's nose.

"Well, make the most of it," said Walter with a spiteful smirk. "My mumsy says it's bringing down the tone of the area, and she's going to get Sergeant Slipper to send them all home."

"Get real, wet brain," said Dennis, flinging his bike into the hedge and climbing over the gate. "This is gonna be the best summer Beanotown's ever had!"

Curly and Pie Face piled over the gate after him, and Gnasher darted through a gap in the hedge, pausing only to nip the heels of the softies.

Dennis made a beeline for the large tent where all the bands were practising. Pie Face and Curly raced after him, puffing and panting.

"Hold on!" gasped Pie Face, as he reached the tent entrance. "I've got about five stitches!"

"That's because you ate five pies for breakfast," said Dennis.

"What are we doing here, Dennis?" asked Curly.

Dennis jerked his thumb over his shoulder into the tent.

"These guys are gonna help us with a brand-new menace," he explained. "The Silver Blades are here, and their drummer is the worst drummer ever."

"So?" said Pie Face as his stomach started to rumble.

"So he's also the loudest drummer ever, and I'm gonna get him to give me some lessons," Dennis explained. "Then I'll get a drum kit – it'll be the best menace ever!"

"I'm starving," groaned Pie Face.

"You guys take Gnasher and find some grub while I get my first lesson," said Dennis.

"Can I help you lads?" asked a voice behind them.

"We're looking for the Silver Blades drummer," said Dennis.

The man behind them looked as if he was in charge. Dennis's mind raced as he tried to decide which menace would get him out of trouble. But to his amazement, the man grinned at him – and it was the grin of a fellow menace!

"I'm Stig," said the man. "I run the festival. Come with me – I'll introduce you to the drummer."

Dennis and Stig strode into the tent. The noise was deafening. Fifteen different bands were practising at the same time. The sound engineers were testing their equipment. Dennis gawped at the speakers, which were about three times his size.

"Brilliant!" he declared.

Dennis came out of the tent an hour later.

"Dennis!" called Curly. "Did you get your lesson?"

"Yeah," said Dennis with a chuckle. "But he said my drumming was a bit loud and he's got a headache. I'm having another lesson tomorrow!"

"This festival's awesome," said Curly. "There's loads of free food!"

"This is the best thing that's ever happened in Beanotown!" Pie Face added. "They've got a stand selling fifty different kinds of pie!"

Suddenly there was a shout from the field gate. A group of people was standing there, and Stig was striding towards them. Dennis, Curly, Gnasher and Pie Face

46

raced after him. Dennis spotted the three softies in the crowd, with their parents. A spindly, pinched-looking man was standing in front of them.

"I demand that you shut this festival down at once!" he snapped.

"Oh really?" said Stig. "Who are you?"

"I am Perkins, the butler up at Deighton Towers," said the man, drawing himself up to his full height (which wasn't very impressive).

"Well, Mr Perkins," said Stig, rubbing his chin thoughtfully. "There are a lot of people here to enjoy the fun, and the festival only lasts three days. I reckon you can cope with that."

"The music is far too loud," said Mr Perkins.

"The field is out of town," said Stig with a shrug. "If people don't want to hear it they can stay at home."

"You're bringing a bunch of muddy, badly dressed, smelly menaces to Beanotown!" roared Mr Perkins.

"And we've got enough of those already," said Walter's mumsy, pointing at Dennis and his friends.

"Thanks for the compliment, Mrs Softy," said Dennis with a chuckle.

"My name is not Mrs Softy!" bellowed Walter's mumsy, looking exactly like an angry hippopotamus.

"We're going to Sergeant Slipper

with this!" raged Mr Perkins. "He'll send you packing!"

"Not a chance," said Stig, folding his arms casually. "We're here fair and square. He can't turf us out for no reason!"

"We'll see about that!" snarled Mr Perkins.

He turned and marched off down the path towards town. Dennis looked at Curly and Pie Face.

"Come on!" he said. "Let's find out what they're up to!"

They grabbed their bikes and followed Mr Perkins and the others into town and up to the police station. As Mr Perkins raised his hand to knock on the door, it was flung open and Sergeant Slipper charged out. He bumped into Mr Perkins and they both fell into the flowerbed.

"What do you think you're doing?" roared Sergeant Slipper. "Obstructing a police officer!"

"I have a serious complaint to make!" said Mr Perkins, removing a tulip from his ear.

"I've no time for you," Sergeant Slipper panted, struggling to his feet. "There's been a burglary at Deighton Towers! Lady Deighton's ruby tiara has been stolen!"

Mr Perkins looked shocked, and then a nasty gleam came into his eyes.

"I bet I know where you'll find the thief," he said. "Up at that festival! They're all crooks!"

"Hmmm, you may have a point," said Sergeant Slipper.

"Don't listen to him!" yelled Dennis. "He just wants to get the festival shut down!"

"Quiet, you menace!" bellowed

Sergeant Slipper. "Someone took that tiara, and I'm going to find the culprit!"

"I suggest that you start with the festival organiser," said Mr Perkins, smoothing down his oily black hair. "He looked like a real menace to me."

Sergeant Slipper set off for the festival field and Dennis glared at Curly and Pie Face.

"We can't let them stop the festival!" he growled. "That bunch of softies just wants to keep Beanotown boring! They don't care who really stole the tiara – they just want to make everyone think Stig's a thief!"

"What are we gonna do, Dennis?" asked Pie Face, searching in his pockets for something to eat.

Dennis stared thoughtfully across the street. The office of the local paper, the Beanotown Gazette, was right in front of him.

"I reckon I'm about to have one of my brilliant ideas," he said.

Half an hour later, Dennis, Pie Face and Curly rode up to the festival field and parked their bikes in a hedge. Gnasher came panting up the path after them.

"Keep up, Gnasher!" Dennis said. "You need to work off all those hot dogs if you're gonna join in the menacing!"

The crowd of protestors was standing by the field gate, while Sergeant Slipper argued with Stig.

"Come on!" Dennis whispered.

They crept up behind the softies and their parents. Dennis reached out and gently pinned a large piece of paper to Walter's mumsy's back. In large, black letters it said:

KEEP BEANOTOWN BORING!

"Quick!" Dennis hissed. "The reporter will be here any minute!"

The three menaces tiptoed around behind the protestors, sticking posters to their backs. Just as they finished, the Beanotown reporter raced up behind them, clicking away with his camera.

"Unbelievable!" he cried. "This'll make a great headline! Is Beanotown boring? Are we all music haters?"

"Certainly not!" said Walter's mumsy, crossly.

"That's not what your posters say, Madam!" chuckled the reporter.

The protestors stared at each other in horror. Their backs were covered in slogans!

"Get them off!" screeched Mr Perkins. "We'll be a laughing stock!"

Dennis cried tears of laughter as the softies and their parents scrabbled and ripped at the embarrassing posters. The reporter was ecstatic.

"This will make a great front page picture!" he whooped. "Parents go Potty! Musical Misery Guts!"

"No one will want to be on their side when they read that!" Dennis chortled.

The reporter took one last snap and then hurried back to Beanotown before anyone could stop him.

"We've saved the festival!" Curly cheered.

"Not so fast!" said Mr Perkins, trampling on the posters and turning to Sergeant Slipper. "I want to make a statement. I saw Stig up at Deighton Towers this morning, just at the time the tiara was stolen!"

"Liar!" yelled Dennis.

"GNASH!" growled Gnasher, hurling himself at Mr Perkins and ripping the seat of his trousers off.

"It doesn't matter what you do!" shouted Mr Perkins as he tried to hide his pink polka-dot underpants. "He's got to arrest Stig on suspicion of theft!"

"You're coming down to the station with me!" said Sergeant Slipper to Stig.

He marched his prisoner away and the crowd started to melt away.

"But he hasn't done anything!" Curly yelled.

"With the organiser in prison, the festival will have to close!" said

Walter's mumsy.

Pie Face opened his mouth to say the rudest thing he could think of, but Dennis clamped his hand over his friend's mouth.

"Urgh, gerroff!" Pie Face mumbled. "Your hand stinks!"

"So does your face," said Dennis, sniffing his hand in disgust. "Come on, we have to prove that Stig's innocent, or else I don't get my drumming lessons and Gnasher doesn't get his free nosh!"

"But how are we gonna prove that?" asked Curly.

"Did you hear Mr Perkins say that he saw Stig up at Deighton Towers about the time the tiara was stolen?" Dennis asked.

"Yea, so?" said Curly.

"So how does he know when it was stolen?" Dennis said. "I reckon he took the tiara just so he could plant it on Stig and get him arrested! And you know what that means?"

"Mr Perkins has won?" said Pie Face gloomily.

"No, you dozy dope!" hissed Dennis. "It means that any minute now he's gonna be creeping into Stig's tent to plant the tiara before Sergeant Slipper gets back to search for it!"

They looked around and realised that Mr Perkins had disappeared.

"Come on!" yelled Dennis.

The three boys raced across the field towards Stig's tent, knocking protestors and festival-goers flying as they ran. One girl let go of her camera as Curly barged past her and it shot upwards.

Dennis turned, spun in the air and caught it with one hand.

"Can I borrow this?" he grinned, running backwards through the mud. "Thanks!"

They reached Stig's tent and Dennis rummaged around in his pockets and pulled out a piece of string. He tied it across the entrance to the tent. Then he pulled a balloon out of his other pocket.

"Grab that tin of red paint over there!" he told Curly. "Quick!"

Curly fetched the paint tin from where someone had been painting the stage. Dennis poured a little paint into the balloon, then carefully blew it up and tied the hole off. Then he heard careful footsteps coming towards them.

"Hide!" he hissed.

The three menaces hid behind the end of the stage – just in time. Mr Perkins came creeping towards Stig's tent. He kept stopping and looking around nervously. Then he put his hand into his pocket and pulled out a glittering, round piece of jewellery.

"That's the tiara!" gasped Pie Face.

"You reckon, brainiac?" growled Dennis. "Shut up!"

Dennis snapped a picture of Mr Perkins as he stepped into the tent, holding the tiara. Then his foot caught on the string and he fell forward with a loud thump.

"Now!" Dennis yelled.

The boys charged over to the tent and Curly hurled the balloon inside. It exploded with an almighty bang and Mr Perkins yelled, then staggered out, covered in paint.

"Caught red handed!" Dennis chortled, snapping pictures as Mr Perkins wiped the paint from his eyes and tried to see where he was going.

"We'll take that!" added Curly, grabbing the tiara from Mr Perkins.

63

"You were the thief all the time!" Pie Face gasped, his stomach rumbling. "Wow, being a detective is hungry work!"

"They'll never believe a bunch of menaces like you!" Mr Perkins sneered.

"You're right," said Dennis. "That's why we made sure we got proof!"

He waved the camera at Mr Perkins as he moved away.

"Come back here, you little menaces!" Mr Perkins howled.

"Better start thinking about the inside of a jail cell," Dennis said. "Because that's all you're gonna be seeing for a while!"

That afternoon, Dennis, Curly and Pie Face handed Lady Deighton's tiara back to her on the festival stage. They were watched by their parents, Stig, Sergeant Slipper, the Beanotown Gazette reporter and all the protestors.

"That dreadful Perkins!" she declared. "Thank you so much for stopping him! You boys are heroes!"

(Dennis's mum fainted in shock.)

"I would like to give you all a month's supply of sausages from the butcher," Lady Deighton continued.

"And I'm giving you each a free pass to the festival," Stig added. "You've earned it!"

"Three cheers for Dennis and his friends!" cried the reporter. "The best boys in the whole of Beanotown!"

(And that was when Dennis's dad fainted in shock.)

CRUISE CONTROL

Afterwards, Mum and Dad admitted that the cruise had been a mistake. But at the time, it had seemed like a really good idea.

"After all," said Dad optimistically. "How much menacing can Dennis get up to when he's out in the middle of the ocean?"

"I don't want to know the answer to that question," said Mum. "But it seems only fair to let Beanotown have a week over the summer holidays without Dennis around. And what could be more fun than a relaxing cruise?"

So they packed their suitcases, left Gnasher with Curly and set off for a week at sea.

At first, everything seemed to be going quite well. Dennis and Bea explored the ship and then they all went up on deck to watch as the cruise ship set off. Then Dennis had a game of table tennis with Dad.

"Perhaps this holiday will be all right after all," said Mum to Bea.

Bea just grinned. Those sounded exactly like famous last words.

The trouble started because of the Kiddy Club. Dennis, Bea, Mum and Dad walked into the ship's lounge and suddenly a loud voice called to them from across the room.

"Hi! Two more wonderful little kiddies to join our club!"

A young woman came bounding over to them. She was wearing a bright pink T-shirt and a pair of white shorts. Her trainers had daisies painted on them, and her hair was tied up in plaits and finished off with pink ribbons.

"Hello, what a lovely little girl!" said the woman, pinching Bea's cheeks.

Bea stared at her in horror and then bit her.

"EEEK!" squealed the woman, snatching her hand back.

"She's . . . er . . . teething," said Mum quickly. "Sorry about that."

"No problem," said the woman, flashing them a huge, large-toothed smile. "But she's just a leetle too young for our club. However, this fine young man is just what we need."

She beamed at Dennis, who lowered his black eyebrows and gave her his fiercest look.

"I'm Melody Dawn," said the woman. "I run the Kiddy Club – a delightful chance for all the children on the ship to have fun playing together – and for Mum and Dad to get a much-needed rest!"

"That does sound good," said Dad.

"I'm not sure that Dennis is qui—" Mum began, but Melody held up a hand to interrupt her.

"Now don't worry about a thing," she said. "Dennis is going to have a simply splendid time with all the children. We have a very special project that they are all going to be working on. Now, Dennis, here is a present for you."

She pulled something out of her pocket, wrote on it and then slapped it on Dennis's chest.

It was a large sticker, which read:

Hi, my name is Dennis.
I'm a Kiddy Club Kid!
Have a nice day!

Dennis couldn't decide what to do first – rip the sticker off, vomit or pelt Melody Dawn with the rotten tomatoes he was saving in his pocket. Dad gripped his shoulder and whispered in his ear.

"Double pocket money for a month if you do this, son," he said.

Dennis looked at Melody. He looked at all the shiny-faced children behind her, wearing their stickers and smiling at him.

"Triple pocket money," he said.

"Deal," said Dad.

Mum, Dad and Bea walked off and Dennis turned to face Melody.

"Come and join us, Dennis," she simpered in a tinkling voice. "We're going to have fun, fun, fun!"

She led the children over to a corner of the lounge. On the other side of the room, Dennis spotted the Captain talking to his senior officers.

"Kiddy Club," snorted Dennis to himself. "Whose stupid idea was that?"

He pulled the sticker off, rolled it into a ball, whipped his catapult from his pocket and shot the sticker across the room, where it hit the Chief Purser on the bottom.

"YOWCH!" he yelled, leaping into the air and clutching his bottom.

"I expect my staff to show some dignity!" roared the Captain. "Control yourself!"

"Sorry, Captain," growled the Chief Purser.

He turned and glared at Dennis, who waved at him cheerfully.

"Now, kiddies," said Melody, clasping her hands together. "We're going to do something wonderful on this cruise! We're going to put on a show for your parents – and you are all going to star in it!"

"Oh, I can't wait!" gasped a blonde, curly-haired girl next to Dennis. "Melody, Melody, please can I have a singing part? My mumsy says that I sing like an angel!"

"Can I be a ballerina?" pleaded the

girl on Dennis's other side. "My daddy calls me his little sugar plum fairy!"

"I'll recite something," said a pompous-sounding boy in a large bow tie. "I'm the best public speaker in my school."

Dennis clapped his hand over his face.

"I'm surrounded by softies," he groaned.

"What about you, Dennis?" asked Melody.

Everyone turned to look at him. Dennis thought fast. No amount of pocket money was worth this – he had to get out of here!

"I'll be a magician," he said, with a menacing twinkle in his eyes.

"Oh, how sweet!" said Melody with another tinkling laugh.

"Can I be your assistant?" asked a

little girl with big blue eyes.

She fluttered her eyelashes at Dennis, who narrowed his eyes and glared at her thoughtfully.

"Yeah," he said eventually. "As long as you don't mind me practising the sawing-a-girl-in-half trick on you. "I've never done it before but don't worry, the saw's nice and sharp."

The girl burst into tears and ran to Melody, while Dennis looked around for a way to escape.

"Let's start by practising the group song," Melody was saying. "I'll sing it through for you first. It starts off:

'We're your darling children
And you love us so.
Now we'll entertain you,
Welcome to our show!'
Now you sing it!"

"Oh, my ears," groaned Dennis. As the children started to sing, Dennis dropped down on all fours and crawled as fast as he could towards the exit. The only thing between him and freedom was a pair of legs in navy-blue trousers.

"Geronimo!" Dennis yelled.

He sprinted towards the trousers, dived between the legs of the Chief Purser and slid on his belly across the polished floor, shooting on to the deck and out of sight. The Chief Purser yelled and leapfrogged into the arms of the Captain, who glared at him and then let him go.

"What is the matter with you today, man?" boomed the Captain.

The Chief Purser saluted and then raced after Dennis, who heard him coming and dashed up the steps to the top deck. Some elderly passengers were having a game of quoits. Dennis grabbed a handful of the rubber rings and hurled them into the group of passengers, hoping to create a distraction so that he could escape. However, he forgot how strong he was and the quoits went sailing over their heads, over the railings and into the sea.

"Quoits overboard!" the passengers shouted.

Several of the passengers, panicked at the thought of a week at sea with no quoits, dived in after them.

"Wrinklies overboard!" yelled Dennis, hurling lifebelts after them.

The Chief Purser blew on his whistle.

"Stop the ship!" he cried. "Passengers overboard!"

The lifeboats were sent after the passengers, and soon they were safely back on board, clutching quoits and dripping wet. Dennis had completely disappeared. The Chief Purser gritted his teeth and clenched his fists.

"I'm going to get that boy if it's the last thing I do!" he snarled.

The following day, Dennis was just sneaking down to the boiler to check for new menacing opportunities, when he heard a tinkling voice that made his blood run cold.

"Dennis dear!" called Melody. "Oh there you are! We somehow lost you yesterday! Come along, we're all going to practise our acts and then sing Kumbaya together."

Dennis rolled his eyes, but he had to follow her. If Dad found out he'd been skipping the Kiddy Club, he'd lose the triple pocket money and be locked in the cabin for the rest of the cruise.

"We might even have time for a group dance," bubbled Melody.

The other children jumped up and down and clapped their hands. Dennis just stared woodenly at Melody, who suddenly looked a little nervous.

"Have you been working on your magic act, Dennis?" she enquired.

"Er, yeah," said Dennis. "I'll just go and get my outfit."

Dennis slipped out of the rehearsal room, charged up the steps and was soon on the swimming-pool deck. He scanned the area for his parents, but they were nowhere to be seen. They had gone off swimming pools after Dennis and Bea had dressed up as sharks in the Beanotown Baths and given the lifeguard a nervous breakdown.

Dennis rubbed his hands together. There were dozens of people sunbathing around the edge of the pool. He spotted an extra-large tub of sun cream beside the pool.

"Don't they know that it's dangerous to go out in the sun without skin protection?" said Dennis, chuckling to himself.

On tiptoes, he worked his way around the pool, squirting sun cream on to the sleeping sunbathers. He made all sorts of interesting shapes and patterns. Soon, everyone was covered in the white cream. Dennis grinned happily, pulled a comic out of his back pocket and went to sit in the shade.

A few hours later, the ship was electrified by an ear-splitting scream. The ship staff raced to the swimming pool.

"My beautiful tummy!" wailed one girl.

"My biceps!" cried a muscly, bronzed man.

The Chief Purser stared around in horror. Every sunbather was covered in peculiar patterns where the sun cream had stopped them getting tanned. Pretty girls had tripe hounds gallivanting on their stomachs. There were insects swarming on arms and snakes slithering up legs. One man looked as if he was wearing glasses, where Dennis had drawn circles around his eyes.

At that moment, Dennis strolled around the corner and doubled over with laughter when he saw his handiwork.

"What an awesome menace!" he spluttered.

"You – I – what – wh—" spluttered the Chief Purser.

"Time to scarper!" said Dennis.

He took a running jump and dive-bombed into the swimming pool, sending a tidal wave of water over everyone. Then he swam over to the other side of the pool, leapt out and sprinted down the stairs. By the time the Chief Purser had wiped the water out of his eyes, Dennis had vanished.

"I'll get that little toe rag!" screamed the Chief Purser, taking off his hat and stamping on it.

"Get a grip on yourself!" exclaimed the Captain, who hadn't seen Dennis. "You're going completely loopy!"

The next day, the Chief Purser got up early and crept around the ship, determined to catch Dennis in the act.

"I'll get him!" he burbled. "If it's the last thing I do, I'll get him!"

He looked up and down. He looked

left and right. He peered ahead. The only place he didn't look was right behind himself, and that's exactly where Dennis was. Just as the Chief Purser started to turn around, Dennis nipped sideways and found himself in the rehearsal room with the Kiddy Club.

"Dennis!" said Melody, clapping her hands together. "George is going to dress up as a cowboy and lasso some toy sheep. Will you put this American Indian headdress on, please?"

She plonked a feathery headdress on top of Dennis's messy black hair. Dennis headed for a door on the opposite side of the room.

"Where are you going, Dennis?" wailed Melody.

"Just going to fetch my tomahawk,"

said Dennis.

He darted out of the room, heard footsteps coming and raced down the corridor. Behind him he heard the Chief Purser give a yell. Dennis skidded sideways so fast that his shoes smoked, and found himself in the gym. He dived behind the equipment and crawled along on all fours. He had completely forgotten about the headdress. As he crept along behind the machines, the feathers brushed against the raised arms of the bodybuilders.

"Tee hee!" giggled the first one, dropping his weights with a gigantic crash.

"Oooh, that tickles!" cried another, letting the bench press smash to the ground.

The gym was filled with the sound of giggles and breaking machinery. The door flew open and the Chief

Purser rushed in. He didn't spot a dumbbell that had rolled towards him, and he tripped over it, flapped his arms helplessly and then somersaulted through the air, landing on the back of a bodybuilder who was doing press ups.

"Arrgghh!" cried the bodybuilder, flinging the Chief Purser off him and on to the rowing machine.

The Chief Purser grabbed at the rowing machine and it catapulted him forwards. He slid across the floor, into the sauna and rocketed into the feet of the Captain, who was having a well-earned rest.

"What the blazes are you doing?" thundered the Captain.

"That boy!" spluttered the Chief Purser. "The boy – in the Indian headdress!"

"There's no boy here!" the Captain roared. "You're hallucinating, man! Pull yourself together!"

The Chief Purser looked around, but Dennis was nowhere to be seen. He groaned and buried his head in his hands.

Over the next few days, the Chief Purser began to wonder if he really was going mad. Someone caused a food fight in the middle of the restaurant. Someone created a riot in the ship's kitchens. And someone put mouse droppings in the honeymoon suite shampoo bottles. But the only thing the Chief Purser saw was the occasional glimpse of a red and black jumper. By the last day of the cruise, he had lost most of his hair and what was left had turned white. As the ship docked back in the harbour, he gazed into the mirror and rubbed his forehead.

"I'm not going mad!" he muttered. "That boy is bound to be at the Kiddy Club show. I'll get him there!"

The parents had all gathered in the lounge for the grand finale of the cruise – the Kiddy Club show.

There were plates of delicious food and gallons of pop on every table. Dennis was backstage with Melody, who was in a bit of a panic.

"Has everyone remembered their lines?" she twittered. "Dennis, is your magic act ready? We haven't seen much of you all week!"

Dennis gave her a grin that would have frozen any Beanotown resident with fear.

"It's all ready," he said. "The greatest disappearing act in the world!"

"It sounds lovely!" gasped Melody.

"It'll knock your socks off," Dennis promised her.

The music started and Melody climbed up on to the stage.

"Welcome, lucky parents of these wonderful, talented children!" she gushed. "Our first act is a young magician with a very special vanishing act. Please put your hands together for . . . Dennis!"

Dennis strode on to the stage and grinned at the audience. At the back of the room, the Chief Purser went purple in the face. He started to gabble and point.

"Shut up, you lunatic!" hissed the Captain.

"But the boy!" whimpered the Chief Purser. "The menace! Something terrible is about to happen!"

The Captain clamped his hand over the Chief Purser's mouth.

"Not another word!" he ordered.

"I want you all to close your eyes," said Dennis.

The officers and the parents all closed their eyes obediently. Dennis reached into his pockets and pulled out a handful of small, see-through pellets.

"Mufumhmmfmm!" said the Chief Purser through the Captain's hand.

The Captain tightened his grip. The Chief Purser stared in silent horror as Dennis's arm swung back, and then threw the pellets across the room like confetti. They smashed against chairs, tables, walls, hats and plates. A choking, horrific stench filled the air. There were screams and gasps as the passengers scrambled for the doors, clawing at each other to escape from the putrid pong. Within ten seconds, the entire room was empty except for Dennis and Bea.

Dennis grinned at his little sister.

"Dunno what they're getting so upset about," he chortled. "Menacing noses can handle a little bit of a smell . . . especially when there's all this free nosh to be eaten!"

"Nosh!" chortled Bea, tipping herself headfirst into a large trifle.

Dennis grabbed a giant bowl of sausage and mash and looked around the room with a contented smile.

"Mum and Dad were right," he said. "Nothing's quite as much fun as a relaxing cruise!"

Collect all ten titles . . .

ISBN: 978-1-84539-098-3

ISBN: 978-1-84539-097-6

ISBN: 978-1-84539-205-5

ISBN: 978-1-84539-214-7

...to complete the menacing series

ISBN: 978-1-84539-095-2

ISBN: 978-1-84539-096-9

ISBN: 978-1-84539-204-8

ISBN: 978-1-84539-213-0

Written by RACHEL ELLIOT

Illustrated by BARRIE APPLEBY

published under licence by

meadowside
CHILDREN'S BOOKS

185 Fleet Street, London, EC4A 2HS

"The Beano" ®©, "Dennis the Menace" ®©
and "Gnasher" ®© D.C. Thomson & Co., Ltd., 2008

Printed in the UK by CPI William Clowes Beccles NR34 7TL